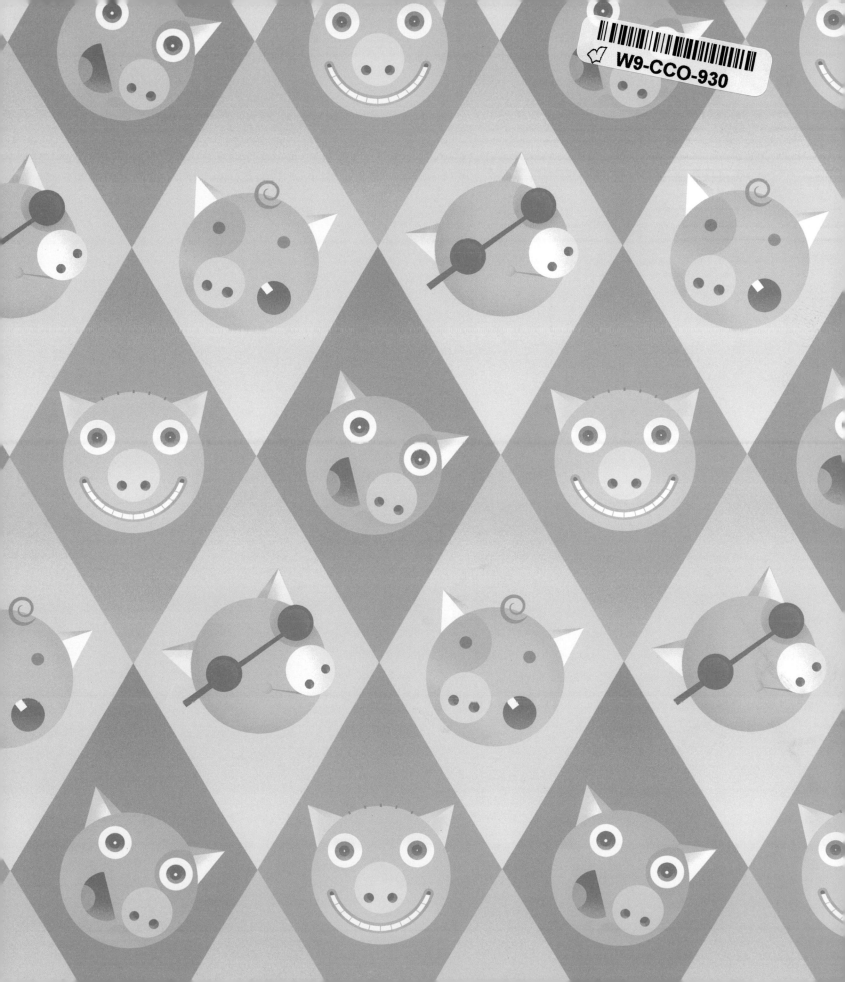

PiGS ROCK!

by **Melanie Davis Jones** * illustrated by **Bob Staake**

VIKING

VIKING
Published by the Penguin Group
Penguin Putnam Books for Young Readers, 345 Hudson Street, New York, New York 10014, U.S.A.
Penguin Books Ltd, 80 Strand, London WC2R ORL, England
Penguin Books Australia Ltd, 250 Camberwell Road, Camberwell, Victoria 3124, Australia
Penguin Books Canada Ltd, 10 Alcorn Avenue, Toronto, Ontario, Canada M4V 3B2
Penguin Books (N.Z.) Ltd, 182-190 Wairau Road, Auckland 10, New Zealand

Penguin Books Ltd, Registered Offices: Harmondsworth, Middlesex, England

First published in 2003 by Viking, a division of Penguin Putnam Books for Young Readers.

1 3 5 7 9 10 8 6 4 2

LIBRARY OF CONGRESS CATALOGING-IN-PUBLICATION DATA
Jones, Melanie Davis.
Pigs rock! / by Melanie Davis Jones ; illustrated by Bob Staake.
p.   cm.
Summary: A music band of pigs plays various kinds of music for their fans.
ISBN 0-670-03581-5
[1. Pigs—Fiction. 2. Musicians—Fiction. 3. Rock groups—Fiction. 4. Stories in rhyme.]
I. Staake, Bob, 1957- ill. II. Title.
PZ8.3.J7535 Pi 2003
[E]—dc21
2002008475

Manufactured in China
Set in Cafeteria, Slappy
Typography by Teresa Kietlinski

To Larry Dane Brimner,
thanks for the inspiration

—M.D.J.

For Al, who brought home the bacon,
and for Jean, who cooked it

—B.S.

Pigs rock. Pigs roll.

Pigs sing with heart and soul.

They sing country.

They sing blues.

Pigs rock with "Blue Suede Shoes."

Fans clap. Fans cheer.

It's the pig rock band they love to hear.

One pig in jeans with leather boots.

The others wear funky suits.

Pigs rock.
Pigs roll.
Pigs sing with
heart and soul.

Pigs play concerts in the park.
Pigs play from noon till dark.
Fans clap. Fans cheer.
It's the pig rock band
they love to hear.

THEATER

O'KEEFFE

OINKY'S

THE SWINEBERG BUILDING

Pigs sleep.
Pigs snore.

Pigs wake up
at half past four.

Down the stairs, out the door,
Pigs hear fans begin to roar.

Pigs wave. Pigs sign.
Pigs leave more fans behind.
Fans clap. Fans cheer.
It's the pig rock
band they love to hear.

Pigs ride. Pigs rest.
Pigs need to feel their best.

Pigs ride. Pigs sleep.
Pigs hear the horn go
beep!

Pigs bounce. Pigs fall.
Pigs make a wrecker call.

Cow Crossing

Pigs moan. Pigs sigh.
Pigs see a truck go by.

Pigs run. Pigs climb.

Pigs rock. Pigs roll.
Pigs sing with heart and soul.
They sing country.
They sing blues.
Pigs rock with
"Blue Suede Shoes."

Fans clap. Fans cheer.
It's the pig rock band they love to hear!

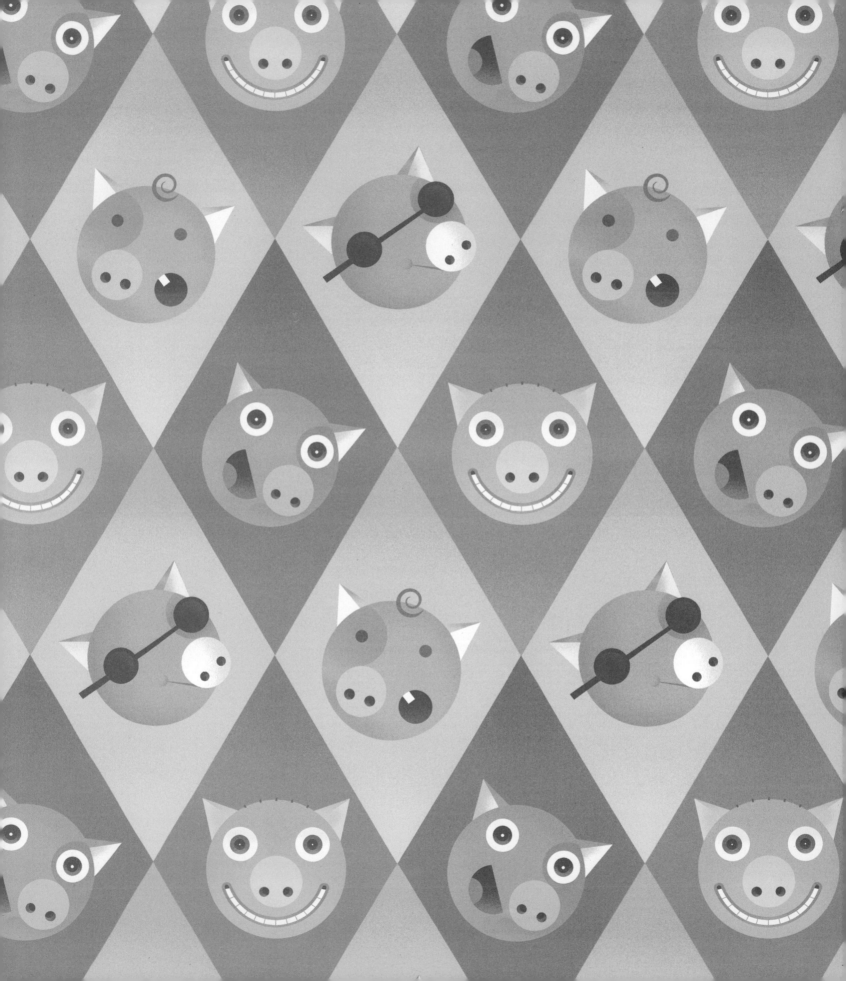